ROAR AND MORE

by Karla Kuskin

NEW EDITION
A HARPER TROPHY BOOK
HARPER & ROW, PUBLISHERS

ROAR AND MORE

Copyright © 1956, 1990 by Karla Kuskin
Printed in the U.S.A. All rights reserved.
New Harper Trophy edition, 1990.

Library of Congress Cataloging-in-Publication Data
Kuskin, Karla.
  Roar and more

  "A Harper trophy book."
  Summary: Rhyming text presents the behavior and
noises of animals such as the lion, snake, and kangaroo.
  [1. Animals—Fiction.   2. Animal sounds—Fiction.
3. Stories in rhyme]   I. Title.
PZ8.3.K96Ro 1990   [E]   89-15650
ISBN 0-06-443244-0
ISBN 0-06-023619-1 (lib. bdg.)

ROAR AND MORE

If a lion comes to visit
Don't open your door
Just firmly ask "What is it?"
And listen to him roar.

ro

The elephant's nose makes a very good hose

Or maybe a holder for flowers.

It can snore, it can croon

Or trumpet a tune.

It has most remarkable powers.

HO O OOOO

OOOOO ONK

This is a tiger
Striped with black.
You snarl at him
And he'll snarl back.

SSNNAA

AARRLLL

The snake is long

The snake is thin

And every year he sheds his skin.

And every year his skin is new.

I cannot say the same

Can you?

H S S S S S S s s s s s s s s s s s

$ $ $ $ $ $ $ $ $ $ $ $ $ $ $ $ $ $ $ $

This animal is a kangaroo.

Well that's not true

She's really two.

One is the Mother

The other is small

Together they run and hop and fall.

Together they wiggle their tails and jump

With millions of noises like wump thrimp thrump.

wamp

THUD

thwamp

bump

Wam

thump

Fishes are finny.

Fishes are funny.

They don't go dancing.

They don't make money.

They live under water.

They don't have troubles.

And when they talk

It looks like bubbles.

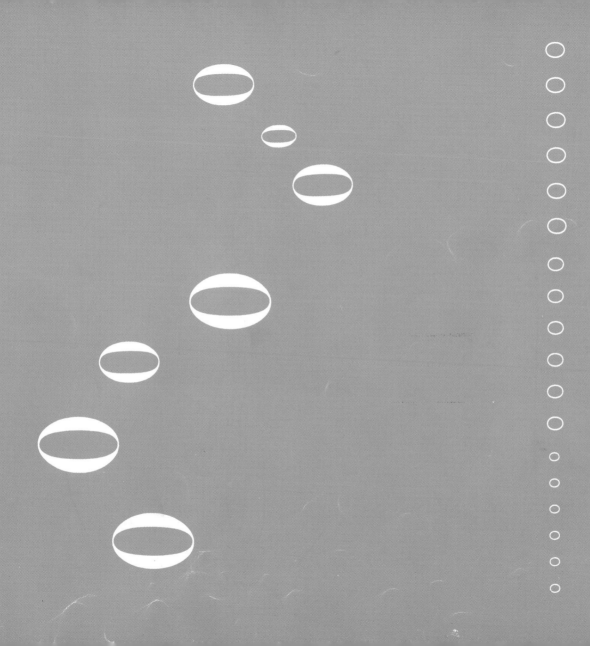

Fish is the wish
Of the cat on the mat.
Or maybe his dream
Is catnip and cream.

PRRRRRRRRRRRRRRRRRRRRRRRRrrrrrrrrrrrrrrrrrrrrrrrrrrr

rrp

The dog has many doggy friends

Who meet him in the park.

They skip on stones

And hunt for bones

And bark and bark and bark.

yap **YAP** yip yip

YAP

WOOF

urf

ARF

GRR

BARK

GRR

rrrRR

bark

BARK

ROWF

YARF

bark BARK

BARK

yip   yap   **YAP**   YAP

Bow Wow   ROWF

yip

urf

ARF   GRRROWF

The bee will choose to spend his hours
Sitting on the ferns and flowers.
So his hair gets full of honey
And his feet get full of fuzz
And his wings when he is flying
Make a fuzzing sort of buzz.

BMMMM Mmmmmmmmmmmmmmzzzzzzzzmzzzzzzzzzz

ZZZzmmmmmmzzzzzzb**zzzz**

Bzzzzzzzz zz Bzzzzzzzzz **Bzzzz** zmmmmmmmmmmmmmmmmmmmmmmmmmmmmmmmmmzz

The mouse runs up the halls

And down the halls

And into walls

And out of walls

He runs most anywhere he pleases

Searching for delicious cheeses.

EEEP

Giraffes don't huff
Or hoot or howl.
They never grump,
They never growl.
They never roar,
They never riot,
They eat green leaves
And just keep quiet.

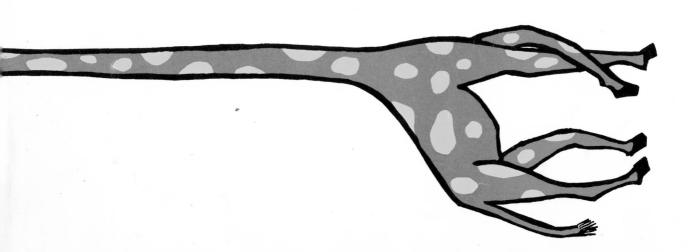

THE END